That Fated Night

SAMSARA-THE FIRST SEASON

A Short Novella of Love & Loss

JL MARTIN

Time Travellers Publishing House Pty Ltd

Also by JL Martin

FICTION

SAMSARA-The First Season

That Fated Night-A Short Novella of Love and Loss

The Golden Glow

Unexpected Beginnings

Torn in Two

Loss of Innocence

Unconditional Love

Returning Home

Letting go

Soul Connections

Healing the Heart

Legacy and Love

Leo-Back to me!

Lilith-Utopia

SPAWNED OF SIN- Trilogy Series

Through Windows in the Sky I Fall

Tainted blood, Poisoned Soul

The Ties That Bind Behind Me

That Fated Night

JLMARTIN

Published by Time Travellers Publishing House Pty Ltd 2021

National Library of Australia.

Cataloging-in-Publication data.

Martin, J L, 1971-.

That Fated Night

Samsara-The First Season

ISBN 978-1-925852-55-4

Cover design by Thea Atkinson

Editing and text design by Marianne Delaforce

Printed and bound in Australia by Ingram Sparks

A Note From The Author

IN READING THE SERIES 'Samsara-The First Season', I ask you to consider the era in which this work of fiction is set. In these more enlightened times, elements of this story may be considered homophobic, racist, and outright morally corrupt—along with being barbaric and downright ignorant. However; in 19th century Australia, they were not. Themes throughout the series are reflective of the times and are an accurate account of the attitude, bias and outright hate a large majority of society held towards the LGBTQI+ Community and our First Nations Peoples. In saying this, we no longer consider it appropriate for a fifteen-year-old girl to marry—forced or not—but 130 years ago, it was not uncommon.

The character of Leo is based on a real person. As outrageous, inappropriate and politically incorrect as he is—I love this soul. It is not my intention to stigmatise him or cause offence to anyone—only to remain authentic in my best effort to honour and immortalise a very dear man who left a significant imprint on my life—and who unfortunately was born without a filter and lacks all sensibilities; and can be very, very badly behaved. Please be aware there are themes of violence, racism, and homophobia throughout this series; however, I have been mindful to write these scenes as sensitively as possible and with the utmost care.

I truly hope you enjoy 'Samsara-The First Season' just as much as I enjoyed writing it.

Dedication

To Mr M Martin

Thank you for your company and comfort during those 3 am starts, and your silence during the endless hours when I needed to work without interruption.
You truly are THE best cat and a role model for the less thoughtful humans that surround you. I love you, Mooksie xx

Chapter One

SHE NAE BELONGS

THE HOARFROST CRUNCHED UNDER the large hooves of the muscular gelding as he snorted, panting heavily, his gait smooth and his footing solid despite the conditions. He followed the well-worn thoroughfare up a sharp incline to the top of the small hill, the town of Edinburgh far behind them. The half-moon hung low as it peeked out from behind dark, threatening clouds, illuminating the boggy road and the sweat-soaked coat of the magnificent horse—its long mane and tail glimmering like black silk on a bright day. The icy wind whipped through the woodland, while the sounds of falling branches could be heard in the distance—a loud cracking sound startling Anna as the wood broke and crashed to the ground and piercing their ears like a gunshot before another rang out only moments later. The scent of the rowan trees was strong despite the frigid winter gale that blustered around them, showing no signs of waning anytime soon.

The rider, shrouded in a thick, woollen cloak that warmed her long legs while skimming her expensive leather boots, the fur-lined hood obscuring her face, carried a wicker basket upon her lap covered with a small blanket, appearing to pay no mind to what lay inside. A petite woman sat astride behind her on the broad back of their steed, her cloak of inferior quality compared to that of her younger sister, whom she had insisted on accompanying on a journey she too had partaken only one year before. The horse came to an abrupt stop, and the small woman gently placed her hand on her sister's shoulder.

'Have ye changed yer mind, Mary?' She pulled her hood back, revealing raven hair bound at the nape of her neck, her bright blue eyes shining as she gazed at her sister. Mary grimaced before raising her hand to push the hood from her own face, her long auburn curls restrained in two thick plaits that fell to her waist, her striking beauty obvious even in the dim light. They stared out over the valley in silence for a time before Mary kicked the horse forward, and they descended the well-worn, uneven track slowly.

'Naw, Anna. I ken 'tis the right thing tae do fer me own sake. Aunt Isabelle has assured me the imp will be weel cared fer, an' 'tis all ye can wish fer the poor wretch. I hope she ne'er finds out she has the de'il's own blood runnin' through her veins.' Mary sniffed while Anna leaned closer and held her a little tighter, tears filling her eyes.

'Lady Isabelle tellt me yesterday me bairn is bonny, an' the Sisters are lovin' an' attentive tae her. I take comfort they'll care fer yer wean as they do me own.'

'Aunt Isabelle needs tae stop tellin' ye anythin' tae do wi' that child. Ye need tae forget her, mo luaidh. I have asked her more times than I can count, but she dinna listen tae anybody an' insists ye have a right tae ken.' Mary shook her head, rolling her eyes as the enormous horse rounded a bend and the imposing orphanage came into view. Anna stared across the distance at the once-grand castle shrouded in darkness, casting an ominous shadow around its crumbling walls and causing the hair on her arms to stand up. As they drew closer, they observed several windows on the ground floor dimly lit by a solitary candle flickering in each one; however, Anna's mind was filled only with the child who no longer belonged to her.

'She dinna speak o' her often, an' usually refuses tae, just like ye. Did she tellt ye they christened her Pollyanna?' she continued, ignoring her sister's obvious irascibility as Mary shook her head and dismissed her with a wave of her hand. She was the only person in the world who Anna could confide in, and although it was kind of Lady Isabelle to bring news of her daughter, they were not as close as the old matriarch was with Mary. 'Lady Isabelle visited Emiliani House only a few days after I birthed wee Polly, as they call me sweet girl. The pur woman was there tae collect the last o' Sister Mary Emeline's worldly possessions, which I heard wasnae much at all. It was Lady Isabelle herself that suggested the name tae one o' the nuns, an' strike me doon wi' a feather, they heeded her. Touched me heart it did that me girl will carry me in her own name fer the rest o' her life. I cannae believe the seasons have turned full circle since I held her.' Tears trickled down her face, a heavy rock of grief sitting in the pit of her stomach as she tried to brush away the memories.

'Dinna fash, me sweet sister. It was fortunate ye secured a position at Merinda Manor after that dreadful business. After all ye have suffered, ye must put it behind ye now. I hope he burns in hell where he belongs, the clatty bassa—an' he can bite me bawsack an' choke tae death, the radge wee shite.' Anna swallowed hard as she tried not to smile, quickly wiping her tears away with her icy fingers, her cheeks flushed and the tip of her nose numb.

'If ye had a bawsack tae choke on.' Anna giggled quietly to herself as they rode on in silence for a time. 'I thank the angels above fer the Harrington family, takin' me in as they did, despite the scandal that followed me. Dear auld Lady Charlotte stood by me, even though me mere presence caused arguments wi' her own blood. I was worrit at one point she would collapse wi' all the kerfuffle.'

'Oh, the Dowager is stronger than ye think, an' much more robust an' canny than she appears. She has been a friend tae Aunt Isabelle fer more than fifty-years, an' that takes courage an' a special kind o' strength an' unwaverin' loyalty in itself.' Mary smothered a smile as Anna giggled to herself. They both adored Lady Isabelle. She had saved them; however, she was a formidable woman who could be intimidating if you vexed her, as they had both experienced over the last year. She had become less tolerant after her daughter, Magnolia Delmont, died on Hogmanay the year just past, having entered the convent at seventeen. She was known as Sister Mary Emeline until she took her last breath and went to be with her God at the age of only fifty-and-five. Lady Isabelle still grieved more than a year later, as if it had only happened yesterday.

Unlike Anna, Mary had chosen not to go into service. She had received the occasional letter over the years, dictated by Anna and written by the head laundry maid where she worked—unavoidable, given she and her siblings were barely literate. She had confided how hard her life was, going into great detail at times, and warned Mary against following her path at the end of each letter, only ever wanting the best for her. They had grown up in the slums of Edinburgh, always dreaming of a better life, but soon lost hope when all they saw around them were people that had more than enough and were still not satisfied. They were acutely aware the majority who were left did not, and never would, have enough of anything through no fault of their own, themselves and their kind included.

Their mother was a hedge creeper, a whore who did not know who fathered her six brats, leaving Anna to help raise her younger siblings—until she ran away at fifteen to work at a grand estate owned by a prominent Scottish family. Mary had taken over their care for the next three-years until she could bear it no longer, leaving only days after she turned sixteen. She was determined to secure a position where she was not enslaved to a master and his hierarchy of servants—knowing full well that the wealthy and those born into privilege held all the power when it came to dictating how those in service spent every waking moment—often without care, compassion or conscience. Mary was also well aware that some treated their servants worse than a beast in the field and valued them far less. She had found Anna within days of leaving the overcrowded city—their bond still strong after not seeing each other for years, while both had grieved deeply every single day that they had been parted. They were overjoyed to be reunited, vowing never to be separated by choice or circumstance from that moment forward.

They had received word shortly after Mary had left Edinburgh that their mother had died. Murdered—or so the rumour went. Their younger siblings had been placed in the workhouse, and although Mary and Anna loved their two sisters, Maisie and Ailsa, along with their brothers, Alasdair and Archie, they did not have the means to care for them. Until meeting Lady Isabelle, they lived from hand to mouth themselves, going to bed many nights with their stomachs growling and living every day with not enough. That had all changed in recent times, and Anna had begun the process of claiming their siblings from the workhouse to care for them herself; although Mary was unenthusiastic and had loudly made herself clear on the matter.

Mary had taken a job in a tavern in the small village at the foot of Castle Leod to be near her sister—finding a sense of peace, despite the long hours she was required to work. However, she felt not a moment of sadness when forced to leave before the year ended when Anna fled in the night to Merinda Manor. Mary had followed her days later and quickly found another position in a tavern in the nearby village, only then discovering why Anna had left so abruptly. Mary had not regretted moving on from her first job, finding she had no time for herself or for Anna.

The elderly tavern owner—a widower who did not enjoy the company of others—demanded she work every day from the early morning till late into the night, shamefully explaining on her first day that he could not spare her, even for a few hours a week. Although the elderly barkeep had been decent enough to her, he was unable to run the place by himself since losing his beloved wife. He did not have the means to hire anyone else, leaving Mary stuck there out of obligation to him and her promise to Anna to always stay close—until she received word from Anna requesting her to come. Mary had rented a room out the back of the new tavern where she was employed, feeling that she truly had a home and a place of her own for the first time in her short life due to her kindly employer and his wife acting as parents towards her and treating the girl as family. Not long after settling into the charming new village, she met Christopher Howard, and life as she knew it changed forever.

Lady Isabelle had helped Anna relocate to Merinda Manor in secret, first making her acquaintance when she arrived back from Australia in the autumn of 1873. She had been invited to stay with a childhood friend, the Baroness of Cromartie, and had graciously accepted, despite receiving a dozen invitations from friends with whom she was closer and would rather have spent time with. During the month she had been a guest at Castle Leod, Lady Isabelle had heard the rumours—and there were many—and sought Anna out one day in the kitchen garden, finding her in a small nook in the courtyard, hidden away where she could stay out of sight of the family while taking fresh air. In no uncertain terms, she had been told by the Mistress of Leod months before she was to remain in her room because of her *shameful condition*, then coldly advised she would offend the respectable people who were forced to tolerate her existence, while not speaking of or revealing her motive or reasoning in keeping Anna at the estate rather than throwing her out onto the street, as was their usual practice when a servant disgraced themselves. On hearing this, Lady Isabelle had taken her hand and led her to a seat, ordering a tray of refreshments she went to collect from the nearby kitchen with her own hands. On her return, she served them both before asking Anna for the truth of the matter, raising each rumour one by one with compassion and kindness.

Anna had denied everything; however, Isabelle had not believed her for a moment and interrogated her at every opportunity over the following days until she confessed the truth. Within the week, she had whisked Anna away to Merinda Manor and arranged a position for her in the kitchen once the wean arrived. As it was apparent she was heavy with child—the loose dresses and aprons she wore no longer hiding her secret—Anna was forced to hide away again. With no husband or father to speak of, bringing unbearable embarrassment and shame to anyone associated with her, she remained in the servants' quarters by choice for a fortnight until the time came to give birth and relinquish her child. Within a week, she had commenced her new position as Mrs Agnes Fraser's assistant, a cheerful woman who had been the head cook at Merinda Manor for decades. The long, painful months leading up to abandoning her child had never been spoken of again once Anna began her employment; well, not in her presence. Only tonight was different.

The horse trudged through the vast, open gates of Emiliani House, Mary silently questioning if the twelve-foot high walls surrounding the castle were there to keep intruders out, or imprison the women and children who lived there, many through no choice of their own. She slowed the horse and moved him towards the rear of the barn that sat on the edge of the large allotment, her heart in her throat at the thought they would be discovered. The horse stopped near a bale of hay left outside and lowered his head to eat.

'Weel, I s'pose this is where he thinks we get off,' Anna whispered, trying to hide the laughter in her voice. Mary silently nodded as she waited for her sister to slip to the ground quietly. Anna raised her arms and took the wicker basket from her, the wean inside sleeping soundly. She placed the basket down on a bench seat that sat looking out over the front of the allotment, then turned back to Mary, who remained atop of the horse, still as a statue, her eyes closed as she murmured to herself. 'Are ye in pain, mo luaidh?' Anna gazed up at her, the moon casting her cloaked shadow across the muddy ground.

'Aye. I'm bleedin' heavily, an' me belly feels as if I've a hedgehog inside fightin' tae get out.'

'Ye should have heeded Lady Isabelle when she warned ye nae two hours ago tae remain in yer bed, an' tae let her organise everythin'—but ye dinna listen, as usual.' Anna stepped forward and tethered the valuable horse to a post, stepping back to admire the beast that Lady Isabelle had gifted to Mary six-months before.

'I got meself in tae this mess. 'Tis up tae me tae get meself out. Aunt Isabelle has been an angel, but

she is an auld woman wi' problems o' her own.'
Anna was puzzled for a moment before a slow
smile spread across her face.

'Ye make her sound like she's feeble an' about
tae go tae God. I've ne'er met a stronger woman
in me life. She puts women decades younger tae
shame. Did ye nae hear what happened wi' the
Applebys?' Mary shook her head before turning to
gaze down at her sister, the mere mention of the
name Appleby piquing her interest. 'Ye will have
tae ask her yerself, as 'tis nae me story tae tellt. I will
say though, I ne'er want tae be at the end o' Lady
Isabelle's sharp tongue, or have her wrath directed
at me. I doubt very much the Appleby's will e'er
cross her path ag'in. Weel, nae on purpose. I believe
they are so frightened o' what she will expose, they
secretly intend tae leave Scotland an' move tae London. Naw yet, but once they can arrange it in the
next few months. If they aren't given the sack first
by auld Lady Harrington herself when she hears o'
it.'

Mary nodded, seeming to have lost interest as she slowly and carefully slid down from the saddle, grimacing as she landed hard on her feet. She placed her hand on her stomach and groaned as she slowly made her way over to the bench. Anna followed, tears in her eyes as she watched her sister bend slightly and pull the blanket down, exposing the sleeping face of the newborn, a shock of auburn hair under her bonnet while she furiously sucked her fist. Mary reached into her pocket and took out a necklace, the emerald stone shining in the moonlight as Anna's hand went to her throat, and she gasped.

'What are ye doin', an' where did ye get that?' Mary placed the precious gemstone around the child's neck, then tucked a note in beside her before pulling the blanket back up and covering her completely. She picked up the basket and straightened her tall frame, tucking it under her arm before pulling her hood back on.

'The necklace is Aunt Isabelle's. Her brother, Ridgley, gave it tae her over seventy-years ago, she tellt me. I have nae idea why she wants this wretch tae have it, as it is clear how much it means tae her. From what I ken, she rarely took it off an' always kept it close. The wee bit I do ken o' her life, I hope it brings this one more luck than it did her.'

'Dae ye think ye will ever come back an' claim her?' Tears filled Anna's eyes again as she looked at the basket containing her niece, her blood, a child who under different circumstances would be hers to love and guide and to watch grow into a beautiful woman—hopefully one with a kind and compassionate heart—unlike her mother, Mary, who often appeared indifferent and cold no matter what the situation. Mary shook her head adamantly, appearing impatient to go.

'Naw. Ne'er. After what Aunt Isabelle has tellt me o' Christopher an' the Howard clan, I want nought tae do wi' him or any o' his spawn. If anybody kens how evil the man is, 'tis her as he is from her own clan. She confided in me only recently that she kent how wicked he was the moment he was born. She dinna explain how, an' I dinna ask, but I believe her all the same.'

'I want tae come back an' get Pollyanna as soon as we are settled in York. The money Lady Isabelle has so generously given will provide a comfortable life fer all o' us—includin' this wee lass.' Anna moved to her side and lifted the corner of the blanket, the wean now awake and staring back into her eyes, tears now spilling down her flushed cheeks. 'Ye dinna even wash the pur wean's face.' Anna shook her head before continuing. 'We now have a modest house all o' our own that nae one can ever take away'. We dinna have tae work if we live carefully on the money in the bank. It'll last at least thirty-years—an' that's livin' weel.'

Mary shook her head furiously and yanked the basket from Anna, turning towards the three sto-ry castle that loomed in the distance. She crept towards the entrance, passing the barn, then the milking shed without glancing back. Anna shivered before quickening her pace to catch up, her new leather boots squelching on the boggy ground. She opened her mouth to speak; however, Mary held her hand up and covered her mouth.

'Haud yer wheesht,' she snapped before releasing Anna, her hand dropping back to her side, the basket held securely on her hip with her other hand. 'The last thing I want is tae be caught here. If ye cannae be quiet, stay here an' wait fer me.' Anna nodded, remaining silent as she slowly navigated her way towards the decrepit building alongside her sister, only the dim glow of the moon guiding their way. After what felt like an eternity, they arrived at the imposing steps of the orphanage.

'Ye must knock hard tae alert 'em she's here. Otherwise, she'll die in this cold. She looked a wee blue afore,' Anna warned as Mary crept up the stairs while she remained a safe distance away. Mary gently placed her burden down in front of the large wooden door without a second glance at the child within, straightening up before gazing down for a moment at the covered basket, the sounds of frantic sucking coming from inside.

'I wish ye all the luck in the world. Ye will need it more than any o' us as yer the spawn o' the de'il.' She turned and knocked loudly on the door several times before gathering her skirt and running down the stairs, continuing across the lawn to a thick hedge, with Anna close behind. They crouched down next to the shrubbery, panting loudly as they tried to catch their breath. Anna turned to Mary, her voice barely audible.

'Dae ye think they heard ye? We cannae wait around all the night in the freezin' cold. The wind is nearly blowin' me off me feet an' on tae me arse.'

'Haud yer wheesht. I see movement in the front window.' Mary remained stone still as they watched the front door slowly open. A young nun holding a lamp stepped outside onto the terrace, raising the lantern above her head to illuminate the front entrance and the endless stairs leading up to it, before noticing the small basket near to her feet. She lowered the lamp and placed it on the tiled floor, then reached across and pulled back the blanket. Gasping in surprise, she stepped away as if someone had pushed her with great force. She was accustomed to finding abandoned bairns on the doorstep; however, this discovery was beyond shocking and had shaken her to the very core. It took several moments before she composed herself, moving back to the basket and bending down to pick up the wean. She efficiently wrapped the child in the blanket that had covered the basket before encompassing her in the folds of her thick cloak. She turned and stared out towards the dense hedge, Anna and Mary unable to breathe as their hearts raced.

'I ken her,' Anna whispered, moving closer to Mary, neither taking their eyes from the young nun who continued to stand on the terrace, gazing out across the grounds.

'I tellt yer afore. Haud yer wheesht,' Mary snapped again. They remained still as they watched the young woman sigh deeply before turning and placing the wean back in the wicker basket. She swiftly gathered it up into her arms and slowly returned to the front door, pausing before turning back towards the front of the property.

'I ken yer out there. Tak' comfort in the knowledge yer wean will be looked after an' loved 'til yer able tae return tae claim the bairn. Please come back when yer life improves an' ye have the means tae care fer yer precious one. I will pray fer ye every night 'til yer return. Go wi' God, an' may the angels watch over ye an'keep ye safe.' Anna tried to swallow the lump in her throat as she watched the nun turn and step inside, closing the door behind her. She glanced sidelong at Mary, who showed no emotion at all as she straightened up and turned to leave.

'Are ye comin'?' Mary stopped to wait as Anna rose unsteadily to her feet, brushing the tears from her face.

'How can ye be so cold an' unfeelin'? Ye dinna even kiss the poor wean goodbye.' Anna hurried to her sister's side, continuing across the grounds and alongside the old barn and shed in silence.

'I will ne'er think o' that child ag'in after tonight, an' 'tis best ye do the same. We now have the means tae live any way we choose—an' I plan tae enjoy every moment wi'out a snotty-nosed succubus clawing at me legs. By the bye, I made a solemn promise tae Aunt Isabelle I will ne'er claim her, or even try tae see her. I even signed a legal contract. She tellt me herself the child was better off at the orphanage than wi' me.' Anna flinched, a pain going through her heart as she watched her sister slowly and carefully climb back onto her horse. Anna swung up behind her with more ease and settled herself for the long ride ahead. 'How do ye ken that nun?' Mary quietly guided the horse through the front gates, her body slowly relaxing the more distance they put between themselves and Emiliani House.

'She's the daughter o' Agnes, the cook at Merinda Manor. I found her tae be a sweet an' very kind lass. She left tae join the Sisters at Inverness as a postulant six-months past. I ken she was born at the estate, an' word is she is a bassa. Her Ma has ne'er named the Da an' is still unmarried tae this day, even though she goes by Missus Fraser. Naw one talks about it either as Agnes is a close friend o' the Dowager an' Lady Isabelle—an' who would dare? I dinna ken anybody wi' bawbags that big.' Mary laughed to herself as Anna shuddered at the thought, the horse quickening his pace as they started up a small hill.

'Did she have tae change her name? I have ne'er understood that.' Mary stared across the rocky croft nestled at the foot of the hill before closing her eyes for a moment.

'O' course. Dinna they all? I ken she was born as Marigold Fraser, but is now ken as Sister Mary Josephine. Lady Isabelle tellt me they all have Mary at the start, then choose the name they wish tae be kent by. I liked her auld name better. It reminds me o' sunshine.' Mary nodded in agreement as she pulled the great horse up at the top of the hill. They gazed down in silence at the dim lights of Edinburgh that flickered in the distance, Mary inhaling deeply before a slow smile spread across her face.

'Weel, mo luaidh. We are free tae leave this wretched place. I have packed yer belongings along wi' me own, an' they are currently on the way tae our new cottage in York, thanks tae Aunt Isabelle. Now, all that's left is tae go an' say our goodbyes tae the few that showed us even a shred o' kindness.'

Anna swallowed hard, fighting back the tears that stung her eyes. There was no more to be said or argued about, and they would start their new life tomorrow on Mary's terms, whether or not Anna agreed. She raised her face to the sky and said a silent prayer before Mary kicked the horse forward, unknowingly leaving behind priceless treasures that no amount of money could buy and they would never find again, in this lifetime or the next.

Chapter Two

AN UNSEEN CONNECTION

T HE HEAVY DOOR SHUT behind her with a deafening bang, the wind whistling loudly outside through the trees and chilling her to the bone despite the thick woollen cape she had pulled on over her habit. She turned and placed her lantern on a sideboard, then slid the bolt into place, securing the ancient wooden doors while balancing the wickerwork box containing the wean precariously under one arm. She then grasped the basket in both hands as she made her way down the wide, draughty hallways towards the nursery, her heart pounding fast in her chest. The wean gurgled as Sister Mary Josephine stared down into her emerald green eyes, shaking her head several times to focus on the child's face, the golden aura surrounding her almost blinding. She should have been terrified, but instead, she was overwhelmed with a deep, almost painful love for the orphan and a strong connection she had rarely felt with any man, woman or child.

She turned into a long hallway, stopping to gaze down at the foundling in wonder. The child stared back, and a smile spread across her lips as her eyes lit up as if in recognition, causing the Sister to gasp in surprise. She was a pretty wee thing, her auburn hair quite long for a newborn and already showing signs it would have a kink to it. Her skin was tinged blue, her face dirty and as cold as the snow on the ground. Josephine frantically ran her hand over the wean's face and body, attempting to warm her as she quickened her step. Within moments, she stepped into the warm nursery, quickly shutting the door behind her. She elegantly moved through the grand room towards the fireplace that ran along an entire wall of what once was the ballroom, her footsteps light and silent in the leather slippers Lady Charlotte had given her the Christmas just passed. A large cauldron of water boiled in the centre of the inglenook between the two sizeable combustion stoves that burned night and day, heating goat's milk for the babies while there was always a kettle simmering away to make tea for the Sisters.

'Sister Mary Marion. Please fill the trough wi' warm water. We need tae warm the wean—an' quickly. She's nae far off frozen.' Her voice was just above a whisper, not wanting to wake the bairns sleeping soundly in the warm, dim room—the only light burning from the hearth and several candles in the windows, while a lamp sat on the table that stood between them.

Marion turned and hurried to the cauldron, bending down to pick up a copper wash basin nearby. She was a sweet soul with unfortunate eyes going in different directions, so you rarely knew where she was looking, but she and Sister Mary Josephine had formed a close friendship, despite Josephine only residing at Emiliani House for several weeks. Marion had been in the nursery for several years now and was considered competent and an extremely hard worker by all who knew her. She placed the basin by the hearth and half-filled it with hot water before taking a large jug and adding cold. She dipped her hand in before nodding to herself in satisfaction, then picked it up and heaved it onto the large table. Josephine hurried to her side with the wean wrapped tightly in her arms.

'Was she on the doorstep like the others? It breaks me heart it does tae see such a sweet wean left tae the mercy o' the world. An' the world is a cruel place beyond these walls.' She gazed down as Josephine unwrapped the bundle, removing her clout and fine clothes before hurriedly slipping her into the water, supporting her head with her hand as she slipped off her heavy cloak with the other and placed it on a chair.

'Dae ye imagine it will be much better inside these walls, now Emiliani House has lost its benefactors? Has only been a month, an' already the bairns' are sufferin'. We barely have enough tae feed the poor souls wi' the snow on the grooned an' nought growin' in the garden. Mr Potts may lose his job, even though he's paid a pittance, an' we would be lost wi'out the man.' Marion nodded as her face filled with sadness.

'Dae ye ken who these mysterious benefactors were? I have me suspicions, but nae one will speak o' it—especially Sister Mary Bernadette.' Josephine shook her head, silently asking the Lord above to forgive her for not speaking the truth. Josephine knew precisely who the benefactors had been. She also knew the reasons they no longer supported the orphanage financially, as one of them had done for over three decades. The other, who had gifted the estate to the church long ago, had also generously supported them—for over half a century—benevolently allowing the children and Sisters to live a comfortable life without worry. 'I have ne'er seen eyes like that on a foundlin'. Have ye?'

Josephine shook her head, remaining silent as she poured the warm water over the tiny child, ensuring she was completely immersed with only her head above the water. Her small face had returned to a healthy pink as she closed her eyes while relaxing back in the water, appearing to enjoy it—far more than any infant they had seen—before turning her head to suck her fist. She had only ever encountered two people before tonight with this strange golden glow surrounding their bodies—one being her mother's dear friend, Lady Isabelle Delmont. She had never told another living soul, terrified she would be cast out as the devil's spawn and disowned by all who knew her, particularly given she was the illegitimate child of a servant. Lady Isabelle carried that aura around her still to this day, and Josephine had noticed just how bright it had been only yesterday when she had visited the orphanage—a visit that had resulted in tears—but not one of them shed by Isabelle.

Marion held out a thick towel to dry the child as Josephine lifted the tiny girl from the water into her arms. She hurriedly wrapped her and moved across to the table that sat to the other side of the fireplace, leaving Josephine to gather her thoughts as she cleaned the mess they had left behind. Once everything was back in its place, she returned to the wicker basket that sat near the door where she placed the wean's clothes and blankets, before turning to ensure the bairns' asleep in the rows and rows of new cots remained that way. Josephine picked up the basket and stepped out into the hallway, placing it on a sideboard, two lamps burning brightly just outside the door. She reached into her pocket and pulled out the emerald necklace that had been around the wean's neck, ensuring she removed it before bathing her or Marion noticed. The emerald was flawless and of superior quality, as was everything on and with the foundling. She reached in and picked up the thick mattress filled with goose down that lay at the bottom of the wicker box, feeling she must hide the valuable necklace for the moment. The young Sister was unsure why such urgency to protect this child gripped her, admonishing herself as her hands trembled and her heart pounded loudly in her ears. Her eyes went wide, and she gasped as a piece of paper dislodged from the side of the basket, fluttering down and landing on top of an official-looking envelope that appeared to have been carefully hidden underneath the tiny mattress, now discarded on the sideboard. She picked up the note and scanned it, finding it did not reveal much. Other than pleading the child be taken care of and, as if an afterthought, a line at the bottom naming her Abigail. Placing the note back inside, she picked up the letter with a trembling hand, her eyes going wide when she saw her name on the front before turning it over to reveal a large wax seal on the back that was unbroken. She slipped it into her pocket just as she heard a distant banging on the front door, startling her as she took out her gold pocket watch the Harringtons had presented to her the day before she entered the convent. She kept it hidden away, knowing if any of the Sisters saw it in her possession, they would take it from her without warning, and she would never see it again. The Dowager then gifted her a silver hairbrush and mirror, along with a pearl necklace that had belonged to her mother-in-law—but not until she transferred back to Edinburgh to join the Sisters of Emiliani only weeks before. Josephine hurried down the hall, winding her way through the draughty passageways until she arrived at the front door, the pounding now louder. She reached up and, with great difficulty, pulled the bolt back and opened the door just a crack, unable to see anyone on the front terrace.

'Who goes there?' She heard footsteps and opened the door a little wider.

'Is that you, Marigold? It's Nellie from Merinda Manor.' Josephine smiled with great affection as she opened the door and welcomed her in. She had known Nellie since birth, and she acted like an aunt to her.

'What are ye doin' here, Nell?' Nellie stopped at the entrance of the door, pulling her cloak tighter around her neck as she shivered, her silver hair bound tightly under her hat. She reached into her pocket and pulled out an envelope.

'I cannot stay, sweet girl. I'm here to deliver this to Sister Mary Bernadette. I don't know what it contains, but it is for her eyes only from the Dowager herself.' She kissed Josephine on the cheek before placing the envelope in her hand for safekeeping.

'Hae ye brought bad news?' Nellie held her by the shoulders, her eyes sparkling as she smiled.

'Of course I have. Is there any other kind at this time of the evenin'? I'm sure you know the Harringtons no longer wish to support Emiliani

House or act as their benefactors.' Josephine nodded, her stomach clenching into knots. 'Well, this just makes it official for all parties, so everyone involved understands the process that is now underway.' Josephine cringed before nodding again.

'Ye ken all hell will break loose once she reads this. I may slip it under her door in the mornin' then run as fast as I can.' Nellie laughed aloud, embracing Josephine again before stepping outside onto the tiled terrace, her elderly body appearing more frail than the young Sister remembered the last time they met. She made haste as fast as her old bones would carry her and was in the carriage and gone within moments, cheerfully calling out her goodbyes while waving enthusiastically out the window long after she was out of sight. Josephine sighed deeply before returning to the nursery, passing the basket left on the sideboard near the door, the necklace and note placed under the small mattress for safekeeping, while the clothes and blankets that appeared to be family heirlooms handed down generation to generation sat folded neatly on top. She crossed the dim, warm room in silence, her mind racing with a thousand thoughts and not one of them making sense.

'Has she made a sound?' Josephine bent down over the child, who was now washed, dressed and wrapped in several thick blankets, a small knitted bonnet placed firmly on her head as she lay in a cot.

'Aye. She belched then farted, but that was all. Such a sweet wee lass.'

'There was a note. The wean's christened Abigail by her kin, so we will honour that an' refer tae her by her own name.'

'Abigail 'tis then. A lovely name fer a lovely lass.' Marion gazed down at the infant, a smile crossing her lips as the babe stared up unblinking into Josephine's eyes, not breaking her gaze for a moment. The women companionably stood side by side, bent over the cot, Josephine gently touching her cheek to gauge her temperature. 'I placed her in wi' Pollyanna as there is nae a spare cot tae be found tonight. I cannae believe just as we lose our bene-factors, there is an increase in abandoned bairns. Unfortunate timin' fer all involved.' Marion shook her head before straightening up and making her way over to the stove. She lifted the boiling kettle from the top and made a pot of tea. Josephine remained where she was, reaching over to Polly to stroke her black, shiny hair—the sweet bairn continuing to sleep soundly despite her touch. The poor child had just passed her first birthday, but was small for her age and sickly. Josephine believed it might comfort the older girl to have the wean next to her, noticing Abigail was reaching out to her and gurgling in a way Josephine had never seen or heard before. She lifted the newborn and placed her close beside Polly, curious to see what she would do. Although Josephine had minimal experience with young children until recently, she knew this child was different from the others. How, she was not quite sure, but she intended to find out.

'Come drink yer tea, Josie. Wee Abigail seems content enough fer now. I will heat some milk tae feed her when she starts fashin'.' Josephine straightened up again as Polly turned in her sleep and reached out for Abigail, taking her tiny hand in her own and clasping it tightly, her sweet little mouth turning up into a smile as she continued to sleep deeply. Abigail closed her eyes and appeared to sigh blissfully, murmuring to herself despite her eyes remaining closed while clearly still wide awake. Josephine covered them with an extra blanket, then made her way over to the small table near the hearth, slipping into a chair beside Marion. She watched in silence as Marion poured from the well-used, elaborate silver teapot while chatting continuously to Josephine in hushed tones. They heard the door open and turned to see Sister Mary Monica hurrying towards them.

'I heard ye found another wean on the doorstep. That's three this past week alone.' Josephine nodded as Monica sat down at the table and poured herself a cup of tea. 'Is she bonny?' Marion smiled, placing her cup back on the saucer before taking a slice of Dundee cake, baked only hours ago by Mrs Murphy, their elderly cook, who became more cantankerous with each passing day.

'Aye, the wee lass is bonny. This one came wi' a name, which is a pleasant surprise they cared enough tae think o' that, unlike so many o' the others,' Marion replied, smiling again at Monica, while Josephine tried to quiet her racing thoughts.

'Why do they bother? These daft hoores' dinna ever return tae collect the results o' their fornication. Nor do they come back tae face their responsibilities an' claim their scabby bassas' tae raise them wi' kin, or suffer the consequences o' their promiscuous behaviour. They're free like the birds in the sky 'cause o' places like this. I doubt they give their blaigeard offspring a second thought once they slither out the front gate on their belly.' Marion appeared thoughtful, confusion crossing

her face while Josephine wondered if she was looking at her or Monica.

'If ye believe they're free like birds tae fly away', why would they slither through the gates?' Monica rolled her eyes at her friend, then raised her hand and spread her arm wide, sweeping it across what was once a grand room that hosted dignitaries, aristocrats and royalty.

'Dae ye think all these fine things we have been provided wi' fer years will last? The blankets will wear thin, the crockery will break, an' there will be naw money tae replace a thing. Mrs Murphy is strugglin' tae feed the children wi'out the butcher an' grocer deliverin' what we need, now we're responsible tae pay fer everythin' ourselves wi' money we dinna have.' She shook her head, anger in her eyes. 'I only entered Emiliani House cause o' the high standard o' livin' for all concerned. Five winters have passed since I moved here, an' now we're facin' an uncertain future.' Marion nodded sadly, reaching over to take her friend's hand.

'I have faith in our Lord that he will provide all our needs. Another benefactor will come along afore we ken it,' Marion reassured her, taking another slice of cake. 'I heard the ruckus yesterday when Lady Delmont was here, an' that ye were called in tae Sister Mary Bernadette's office. Why?' Monica grimaced, her face like thunder.

'Dae nae speak tae me o' that maleficent trollop. I have been warned by Bernadette nae tae repeat a word o' it, or she will have me hide an' ne'er speak up fer me again. I will tell ye this, though. That malevolent woman destroyed me family, an' is now tryin' tae destroy me. She's doin' everythin' in her power tae have me cast out on the street an' me reputation ruined.' She shook her head in disbelief, her body shaking while her hands curled into fists on her lap. 'Me great-grandfather was the highly respected Judge John George Maslow, an' she placed a curse on him an' two o' his friends long afore I was born. They all met a horrible death one after another in the years tae follow, but me poor

Grandy suffered the worst o' 'em all.' She quickly wiped away tears that threatened to spill down her cheeks.

'Aye. I heard about that when I was a wee bairn meself,' Josephine remarked as Monica turned to her, her eyes blazing.

'Aye, o' course ye did. Those Harringtons an' yer Ma need tae be careful who they choose tae be friends wi'—an' so do ye, Josie. I cannae associate wi' ye when ye look towards the evil witch as an aunt. She is Beelzebub's own daughter, an' mark me words, ye'll regret the day ye met her.' Josephine ignored her and raised her cup to her lips, gazing over at the wood crackling away in the hearth—the flames dancing in orange, red and blue, and reminding her of the kitchen at Merinda Manor—a place she missed dreadfully. The Harringtons had always been good to her mother and herself. They treated them as family, unusual given no other servant was on familiar terms with any of them, nor with Lady Delmont. She was a constant guest of the Dowager, staying at the manor often when in Scotland, despite owning an estate near Inverness and a grand castle in York near her family home, Castle Howard. Josephine had struggled to get along with Monica from the day she arrived at Emiliani House, as somehow, she had been made aware of her connection to Lady Delmont and taken an immediate dislike to her. Neither Josephine, nor her mother, were acquainted with the Maslow family; however, many were, including the Harringtons, as they were a prominent and influential family from England who spent half the year at their estate in Scotland not far from the Harrington estate.

'We must think an' speak o' others wi' love, Monica, an' pray fer their souls no matter what their perceived sins,' Josephine reminded her quietly, unable to meet her gaze. Monica finished her tea and turned to Josephine, her lips curled up into a sinister smile.

'I will speak as I please,' she snapped, glaring across at her. Josephine raised her chin and held her head high, despite her insides shaking and an overwhelming desire welling up from deep in her belly to flee back to Merinda Manor and never set eyes on Monica again in this life or the next. 'As fer them Harringtons, do they think we are deaf, dumb *an'* blind? Anybody wi' half a brain kens that auld Lord Reginald gave this estate tae the Sisters o' Emiliani, an' that his wife, the Dowager, took over when he died. 'Tis on record in Bernadette's office that he gifted the place tae us in the 1830s, as it was an unwanted weddin' present from his parents—ungrateful auld sod he was. I ken he provided an adequate amount o' money each month tae feed an' clothe us all, but 'tis her that made the decision tae abandon the bairns an' us selfless women o' God an' leave us destitute an' starvin'. Her son is the Laird now, an' he should continue tae be the benefactor, whether she likes it or naw. As fer the other benefactor, he has tae have some connection tae the Harringtons an' wi'drew his support at their direction.' She raised her nose in disdain as Marion made a fresh pot of tea. Josephine swallowed hard, finding it difficult to hold her tongue. Lord and Lady Harrington were kind and gentle souls, and it had devastated Josephine when he passed, as he had been a grandfather to her. His heir apparent, Lord Reginald Harrington II, was very much like his father and was kind and sensible, and very much well-liked and respected in the district. He had married late in life, and after years of trying to produce an heir, his wife bore him a son only five-years ago—a sweet boy called Reg, or Lord Reginald Harrington III, whom Josephine was fond of and missed dreadfully.

'Weel, it was a kindness from the auld Duke so generously givin' this place over tae the kirk, God rest him. A very kind gift indeed, whether he appreciated it himself nae matters. We must concentrate on the good in the world, Monica, nae the evil that seems tae always be lurkin' close by, waitin' fer ye tae leave the door open an' invite it in,' Marion warned as she placed the pot of tea on the table with a creamery jug filled with fresh milk and a bowl of sugar.

'I ken fer a fact that Isabelle Delmont has somethin' tae do wi' the Dowager wi'drawin' her support. Isabelle only ever cared about this place when her scabby bassa daughter lived here. The day that blaigeard Emeline went tae the pits o' hell was one o' the happiest days o' me life.' Marion and Josephine gasped as Monica wiped the spittle from her lips, her face purple and her hands shaking in anger.

'Sister Mary Monica! Haud yer wheesht afore ye are struck down by lightnin' where ye sit!' Marion warned as she shifted in her seat, then raised her eyes to the ceiling and said a silent prayer before crossing herself and nervously nudging her chair closer to Josephine. Josephine raised her hands and placed her palms on her burning cheeks. Closing her eyes for a moment, she prayed for Monica's soul, along with asking for forgiveness for wanting to kick her hard under the table until she bled and her shin bone was broken in several places.

'I willnae haud me wheesht, Marion! Ye out o' anybody ken she was a bufty wifie as well as I do. She should have been cast out o' here the moment she arrived all those years ago when they found out what she was. She was nae bride o' Jesus or the Holy Father. She was the bride o' Mary Magdalene in thought, word an' deed—an' let's nae forget the poor Sisters she corrupted over the years wi' her filthy inclinations.'

Josephine felt tears sting her eyes as she tried not to show any emotion. Monica was the reason Sister Mary Emeline had taken her own life after she had exposed a long-standing love affair between her and Sister Mary Teresa, whom she had met as a postulate nearly forty-years before. They had lived side by side, sharing a dormitory, harming no one, and although some had speculated on the true nature of their close friendship, they soon dismissed their suspicions, as all that met Emeline loved her—except for Monica.

It had taken Lady Delmont over a year to find out why her only child had committed the ultimate sin against a God she so loved and hung herself in the milking shed that dark night—no doubt the reason for her attendance yesterday and the skirmish that followed in the office. Emeline had sent word a year before her passing, asking her mother to return from Australia as she was feeling poorly and had been for some time. Emeline had never been sick a day in her life and had not known where to turn when Sister Mary Monica discovered her secret, knowing the only person in the world who could protect her and Teresa was her beloved mother. Josephine had heard whispers recently from a friend, a scullery maid at Merinda Manor, who was more than happy to relay the latest gossip going around the estate during her weekly visits to the orphanage. She confided she had overheard Lady Delmont tell the Dowager last week that she had only recently discovered Sister Mary Monica had been blackmailing Emeline for over two-years. It was rumoured she had been forced to complete all of Monica's chores along with her own and ordered to hand over the modest allowance her mother sent to her each month in return for Monica's silence. Once Lady Delmont arrived back in Scotland several months before that dreadful night, Emeline refused to tell her of her situation, no matter how much she prodded and probed. Emeline had not wanted to burden or anger her into taking action against Monica or the Maslow family, jeopardising her position and reputation within the convent. She knew her mother's temper and disposition intimately, along with her loathing and contempt towards anyone who carried the name Maslow. Emeline also knew better than anyone just what her mother was capable of when anyone she loved was threatened or harmed, and she was a formidable enemy to have if you were so unfortunate—or simpleminded—to betray or cross her.

No one knew what caused Monica to go to Sister Bernadette and Bishop John Menzie-Strain a few days after Christmas, or what they discussed. However, days after that conversation, Sister Mary Emeline and Sister Mary Teresa were summoned to appear before the Archdioceses in Edinburgh. Teresa never returned to Emiliani House after the Bishop allowed them to leave once the meeting had concluded, and her whereabouts were unknown still to this day. Some believed she fled back to Ireland, others were certain she took ship to Australia. Still, the hierarchy within the Catholic church didn't seem to care one way or the other, relieved the situation had resolved itself without further intervention or embarrassment, permitting them, with a clear conscience, to never speak of it again. Emeline had returned alone to Emiliani House that same afternoon and locked herself away in the dormitory that she once shared with her love, now alone for the first time in nearly four decades. The Sisters did all they could to coax her out as she was dearly loved by them all, most unaware of what had occurred or what the true nature of their friendship had been, but she refused and remained alone with her memories. No one heard her later that night when she crept out to the milking shed, and when found the following day, shock and grief lay heavy on all that knew and loved her—except for Monica.

'Weel, ye *need* tae haud yer wheesht afore I push ye out o' this room meself. Ye are just bein' cruel now, Monica. Tae speak ill o' the dead—weel, 'tis naw right, an' I ken in me heart an' soul yer better than that.' Monica gazed across at the hearth, remaining silent as Josephine attempted to hide the contempt she felt for this woman who was her sister in Christ, yet was the devil incarnate.

'Show me the new wean afore I go an' find me bed, then. 'Tis gettin' on tae midnight.' Monica yawned loudly, not bothering to cover her mouth as she rose to her feet, while Josephine remained where she was and poured herself a fresh cup of tea, adding milk and sugar while they still had it to enjoy. Marion led her over to the cot, placing her finger to her lips to ensure Monica remained silent and did not wake the sleeping bairns.

'Is she naw bonny?' Marion whispered, smiling down at the sleeping babe, her tiny fist entangled in Polly's hand as they lay side by side, not a slither of space between them. Monica narrowed her gaze as she leaned down over the cot.

'I cannae believe she favours that imp, Emeline. If I dinna ken she were cold in the ground, I would bet me life this child came from her loins. Mist be 'cause we spoke o' the wicked soul, an' now I cannae shake her memory.' She continued to gaze down at the sleeping wean; however, she refused to touch her, suspicion in her eyes as she studied her sweet face closely and the wisps of auburn hair escaping her cap. She glanced over at Polly and sighed deeply, briefly reaching over to stroke her raven hair before straightening up.

Josephine refused to continue to listen to the hate that spewed from her mouth and rose from the table unnoticed, hurrying across the room and out into the hallway to hide the wicker basket and its contents, fearing the conclusions Monica would undoubtedly come to should she see the costly items, or read the note that had accompanied wee Abigail. She placed the basket in the cupboard under the stairs before turning back to make up a bed in the nursery for herself. Sweet Marion would be glad of the company, Josephine was sure, and she realised at that moment, she would not return to the dormitory she shared with three others—not next week, next month, or even next year. She had no choice but to remain by Abigail's side, the desire to be near her so intense, she felt physical pain in her heart when parted, while feeling a joy so profound when close to the wean.

One thing she knew for certain was she had been sent here to love and protect that child. She did not understand the why, who and how of it all, nor did she know where wee Abigail came from, or who she belonged to. It made no difference, nor did it even slightly diminish the infinite love that immediately and without warning filled her once empty heart at the first sight of the child. In the absence of the wean's own kin, and from that moment on, Sister Mary Josephine claimed the child as her own—a commitment she would honour until she took her last breath—no matter what the cost or the consequences.

Chapter Three

HELL HATH NAE FURY

CHARLOTTE STEPPED INTO HER private drawing-room, her ladies' maid, Nellie, following close behind. She smiled before making herself comfortable on the oversized wingback chair near the fireplace, indicating with her hand for Nellie to sit down next to her on the identical chair that was once her husband's—a low, gilded table sitting between them. The warm and comfortable room had been provided for her to use as she wished by her dearly departed mother-in-law over half a century ago. She had felt emotional when she first arrived from Australia to marry her betrothed, Lord Reginald Harrington—a man she had not seen since childhood—but meeting Lady Isabelle on the ship in Sydney and becoming firm friends almost immediately had helped ease her nerves. Charlotte had been sick with fear and dread during the voyage regarding what she would find on her arrival. She only had a vague recollection of the Harrington family from when she was a wee lass before her family immigrated to Australia, and from those faint memories from so long ago, she could not form an opinion one way or the other to ease her fears. On her arrival in Scotland, she found his parents, the Duke and Duchess of High-grant, to be kind and welcoming, relieving her anx-iety immediately after they embraced her as their own within the first week. Reg's mother had kept the large drawing room towards the front of the manor until the day she took her last breath nearly thirty-years earlier. Although this room was much smaller, it was just as elegant and lovely, decorated in a soft peach and cream palette with beautifully made rugs covering the floor, just as it had been the day she first stepped into the room. She was fastidious when it came to redecorating the entire manor every ten-years; however, she ensured this particular room remained as close to what it had been when she first made Merinda Manor her home. This was the one room in the entire residence where she had complete privacy and could stay out of everyone's way now that her son and his wife were the new Duke and Duchess of Highgrant—promoting or demoting her, depending on your perspective—to the Dowager of Highgrant now her beloved Reg was no longer by her side.

The fire burned warmly in the hearth while Charlotte and Nellie relaxed side by side in front of the fireplace, Nellie only having just returned from delivering a letter to Emiliani House on behalf of the Dowager. She was relieved to be back as the night was cold and stormy, the wind so strong it could knock down a hairy Sasquatch. They were startled by a knock on the door, the new butler nodding politely before stepping into the room with a tray holding a bottle of wine and two crystal glasses.

'How kind of you, Mr Masters. I can always rely on you to take care of me without even asking. Thank you.' He nodded in acknowledgement as he poured the Dowager a glass of wine, then did the same for Nellie. He was the youngest butler Merinda Manor had ever employed, and by far the most efficient in Charlotte's opinion, based on previous experience with those who had come before him. She often had to remind herself he was only a lad at one and twenty, despite appearing old for his years in mind and mannerisms, while outwardly, he was formal to the extreme, irritating her at times. He came highly recommended by a friend of her late husband, who had employed his father as their butler for nearly four decades. 'Please join us in a nightcap. There are spare glasses on the buffet.' Mr

Masters nodded obediently, although clearly uncomfortable as he crossed the room and retrieved a crystal flute before returning and pouring himself half a glass of wine, taking a seat opposite the Dowager.

'I do need to speak with you in private, Mistress. The matter is of an urgent nature.' Mr Masters sat straight as an arrow, the deep ruby wine in his glass untouched.

'You can speak freely, Mr Masters. Nellie has been with me for half a century and is my friend and confidant first and my ladies' maid last. Anything said in this room will remain here.' Charlotte smiled at him in an attempt to help him relax; however, she failed spectacularly as he straightened up even further in his seat and placed his glass on the table beside him, his tall, slim body now tense.

'As you wish, Mistress.' He nodded his head slightly before continuing. 'It regards Anna Campbell, the cook's assistant.' He paused as Lady Charlotte nodded.

'I am aware of who she is. Please continue.'

'I received her notice today. She has decided to move to York with her younger sister. She would give me no further information, but I expect she is leaving because of the scurrilous rumours that are still being bandied about without thought or care, not only by the servants in your employ, but also around the village from people who have never met her. Now there is talk of her sister, Mary, that is not fit for your ears. I find it all very sad they forced her out, Mistress, as she is a lovely young woman.'

'Yes, she is. Unfortunately, I cannot protect her, or her sister, from gossip; nor can I intervene, as that would only make things worse. Tell me what you have heard.' The uptight butler swallowed hard several times, appearing reluctant to continue, his face flushing slightly.

'There are several rumours I have heard, unfortunately, and not one of them is complimentary.' He swallowed again, quickly running his tongue over his dry lips. 'There is talk that the child she bore was sired by a married man at Castle Leod, the seat of the clan Makenzie.' Charlotte raised her eyebrows as she narrowed her gaze.

'You mentioned several rumours. Tell me of the others.' She leaned back in her chair and crossed her arms against her chest, waiting for him to continue. At times, she felt like shaking the man, while fighting an overwhelming urge to mess up his immaculate hair and uniform just to see how he would react, but she restrained herself daily and behaved as expected.

'That rumour seems to be the most popular. There was talk she was selling herself down in the village to make extra money to provide for her siblings that are in the workhouse,' he replied, pausing for a moment and swallowing hard before reluctantly continuing, his cheeks now a deep purple, 'and that the child she carries was fathered by one of her customers.'

'Well, that's an outright lie! It really is no one else's business who fathered that poor wean, and the subject is best left alone. Please pass this on to all who work and visit here if it is mentioned again. I will find and chastise those who are behind this, mark my words. God help them if Lady Delmont hears of this. She loves that girl and her sister as if they were her own blood and has provided for them accordingly. You can repeat this to all that will listen. Anna has made a new life in York, at the insistence of Lady Delmont and with her financial and emotional support, as it is far too painful here for her to endure. As for the other hundred rumours, I do not wish to hear any more of them. That's the end of it!' Mr Masters sat back as if someone had slapped him, his eyes going wide for a moment before he nodded and rose to his feet.

'As you wish, Mistress. Is there anything else I can do for you before I retire for the night?' He stood erect and unmoving as if made of stone, waiting silently for her direction.

'You may go, Mr Masters. Thank you for informing me of the current situation here at the manor. I feel like I am left out of everything these days, and it's comforting to know you will always keep me up to date, as the young ones say. Thank you, and sleep well.' He bowed low before placing another bottle of wine on the small table between Charlotte and Nellie, bowing again before stepping away and bidding them both goodnight, then hurrying out the door before either had a chance to reply. Nellie giggled softly, turning to Charlotte and raising her eyebrows suspiciously.

'You never denied that first rumour,' she remarked mischievously as Charlotte shook her head and smiled.

'I cannot deny or confirm anything I do not know for certain, can I, my darling Nellie? Dear Isabelle told me of the situation she encountered when staying with the Baroness of Cromartie. Her great-nephew, Colin McKenzie, is just one of several men from Castle Leod suspected of fathering the wean.' Charlotte paused for a moment to take a deep drink of her wine, draining the entire glass before she settled back in her chair, moving a stray silver hair from her weathered face. She rarely bothered standing in front of a looking glass these days. She no longer recognised herself compared to the elegant blonde beauty she had once been, now finding those around her often looked straight through her as if she no longer existed in the physical world. On the other hand, Isabelle was still strong and beautiful; her skin barely wrinkled at all and her hair still thick and glorious without a single strand of silver to be seen.

'Why is it such a scandal? I have no doubt Isabelle could find and force the man to do the right thing and marry the poor girl. We all know what an abominable force she can be when she sets out to right a wrong, or pursues a person she believes has injured or threatened her or someone she loves. It will undoubtedly help restore the girl's reputation if the man is identified and forced to marry her. They can then claim back the wean from the orphanage and, given time, most will forget and move onto the next titillating impropriety that some poor soul unwittingly commits.' Charlotte shook her head again as she laughed sarcastically, screwing up her nose in disdain.

'Did you not hear what Mr Masters said? It's a scandal because in that particular instance if Colin Makenzie is indeed the father, the bastard is already married and has three young bairns—twin boys who are barely five, and a wee lass just gone two. I have met young Colin a number of times over the years, and his long-suffering wife Harriet, who is a dear, sweet soul and far too good for him, in my opinion. The poor woman should have stayed in England with her own kin, where she was once happy. From what I have heard and witnessed in recent years, he will never remain faithful to any woman, no matter how beautiful, clever or wealthy. That man could not keep his cock in his pants if his life depended on it. I'm not saying he is the father, as there have been whispers regarding one of his cousins and an uncle who is rumoured to have taken Anna by force. No one knows, and Anna will not speak of it. No, Anna is far better off moving away and forgetting about the man at Leod who she refuses to name, along with the child she bore as a result.' Nellie shook her head sadly, the deep lines across her brow and near her eyes causing her to look just like her granny when she was nearing the end of her time on earth. But, oh, they had lived and done it with grace and style. Neither had any regrets as they had spent nearly their entire lives together—first as Mistress and servant, but as the years passed, they settled into a close and comfortable friendship.

Nellie nodded, gazing around the room and admiring the small, carved desk dear Charlotte used when writing her correspondence, containing the finest furniture that could be found not only in Scotland but down to London and across to Wales and back again. No place was too far if Charlotte came across a piece of furniture or art she adored, sparing no expense or concern regarding transporting her treasures across the country or by sea. The heavy drapes were open as they sat in companionable silence, gazing out into the darkness, the wind whipping through the trees at an alarming speed while the night was frigid, with ice on the ground. It had been bitterly cold in York when Charlotte accompanied her dear friend Isabelle to visit her family a fortnight ago; however, there was no comparison when it came to a Scottish winter. Charlotte had always loved Scotland, especially in the coldest season of them all, when the trees and mountains were covered in snow—a sight truly spectacular to behold. She would enjoy the view and all its beauty through the floor to ceiling windows of her drawing-room, staying warm inside the protective walls of the manor she had grown to love. Unable to forget the unbearable heat of Sydney town she was forced to endure all those years ago, she had not once regretted her decision to return home without her family, who had all gone to God now, just like many of her friends she had loved for a lifetime. She was a realist, and now she was well into her seventh decade on earth, keenly aware she was winding things up after a magnificent life well lived, accepting with grace she too would soon take the stage for the last time to make her final bow. Charlotte finished her wine before Nellie reached across and refilled her glass, topping up her own, then placing the empty bottle back on the table.

'I think it's so sad for the bairns, who will never know where they came from or whose blood runs through their veins,' Nellie murmured, almost to herself.

'I agree with you. That was why when a similar situation occurred within these walls, I did inter-vene, although not a soul knew about it at the time.' Nellie widened her eyes mockingly before she laughed aloud.

'How's that possible in a place like this? There are hundreds of people living and working here, and nothing goes unnoticed, let me assure you. I hear everything.' Nellie took another sip of her wine as Charlotte stared at her for the longest time.

'Well, I am confident you do not know that Agnes and my son were lovers for several years before he married. He fathered young Marigold Fraser—now known to you all as Sister Mary Josephine.' Nellie choked on her wine, coughing and spluttering as Charlotte reached over and pounded her on the back, smothering a smile. She continued to gasp for air, clutching her throat until it had passed and she could compose herself, accepting the glass of water gratefully that Charlotte handed to her before taking a sip.

'How did you hide that? It's not a small secret to keep.'

'The only way secrets are kept is if people do not discuss them, ever.' Nellie turned to her, reaching across and taking her hand in her own before squeezing tightly.

'Who knows? Obviously Agnes and young Reg, and of course, you. And now me.' She smiled sympathetically across at her dear friend, her employer—a kind and compassionate soul who had ensured her life was just as comfortable and secure as her own. A woman who had not once in all these years treated her as someone beneath her when most in her position would without guilt or a second thought. Charlotte remained silent for a time, deep sadness filling her eyes.

'I suspected long before Marigold was born, my son and Agnes were involved in a deep and passionate relationship. I believed them to be a good match when Reg came to me in confidence and told me of his love for her; however, my husband was from a different world where titles and class are more important than the air you breathe, as you well know. He demanded our Reg finish it with Agnes and find a suitable wife, which he did reluctantly and with a shattered heart. Months later, Marigold was born, and I knew she was my grandchild, but I never told my husband, or he would have thrown them out on the streets of Edinburgh and left them to beg; although, I suspected in later years he knew the truth by how he treated our dear Marigold.' She quickly wiped a tear from her eye before sniffing loudly. 'Agnes was loyal and steadfast, remaining silent on the matter to this day, as I expected from such a generous soul with such a pure heart. Her love for my son is as deep as the ocean and as vast as the universe, reaching beyond this life to the next, and I know for certain my son feels the same way about her. Reg does not speak to me of it anymore, preferring to leave the past in the past now Marigold is grown and leading her own life.' She leaned forward and picked up a pipe, filling it with tobacco from her late husband's leather pouch. 'There are two others that know the truth, but I am confident they will never speak of it.' Nellie waited silently as Charlotte lit the pipe and inhaled deeply, until impatience overwhelmed her, and she could wait not a moment longer.

'Well, tell me who? Just open your mouth and let the words flow, and stop making me wait. This would be the most interesting scandal you have ever shared with me, and now you want to take your time,' Nellie teased her, moving her chair a little closer.

Charlotte gazed out the window to the left of the room that looked out onto the hothouse, as she liked to call it—the magnificent glasshouse built not long before she arrived so long ago now. The head gardener cultivated their vegetables, herbs and several varieties of fruits inside the glass building—many of the seeds and cuttings provided by Castle Howard, an estate well known for producing the widest varieties of fruits and vegetables in all of England.

'See the glasshouse out there?'

'The conservatory?'

'Oh, stop being fancy. You know what I'm talking about.' Charlotte rolled her eyes as Nellie smirked at her and nodded so she would continue. 'I was out there one day, years ago now, when Marigold had just turned seven. She had celebrated her birthday the day before and came looking for me to show me her presents. I had been feeling melancholy, not being able even to embrace the poor child, and I was suffering deeply, unable to confide in a soul to ease my torment. She came strolling up to me and asked why I was hiding behind the hothouse, telling me she also found it far too warm to stay inside for more than a few moments. I looked into her eyes and couldn't stop myself. I told her I was sad because I was her grandmother and wasn't allowed to tell her.' Nellie wiped tears from her face with her handkerchief before loudly blowing her nose.

'I want to know more, but I don't. It's all too sad.' She sniffed again as Charlotte reached over and took her hand.

'No. It's not sad at all. It was heartbreaking before Marigold knew the truth. After I broke down and told her as much as was appropriate for her tender years, the sweet little angel wrapped her arms around me and promised she would never tell a soul. To this day, she has not even told her own mother that she knows who her father is, or that Reg and I are her grandparents. We treated her as our own as she grew, and she loves us deeply, knowing we belong to her just as she belongs to us.' Charlotte wiped her face and straightened up in her chair, smoothing down her skirt before exhaling.

'Why would you withdraw your support as a benefactor to Emiliani House when your own grandchild resides there and will live in poverty in the not too distant future?'

'That is a long story, and not one I am ready to tell tonight. Complex circumstances arise without warning quite frequently during a lifetime on this earth, often through no fault of our own. It draws you into the chaos without a choice in the matter—if you have any sort of conscience. I myself have been placed in situations that have left me with no alternative but to speak up against injustice, and unfortunately, it is often unavoidable that you upset and enrage those you have challenged. Some become so incensed and offended when they are told things they are not ready or willing to hear, escalating to the point of violence if they feel threatened, while often becoming even more belligerent and stubborn if they refuse to concede and rectify their behaviour. I find it even more disappointing that most do not intend or attempt to make amends for their poor choices and actions that have impacted others in unforgivable ways. Emiliani House and the Archdiocese need to be held accountable for the sins they have committed, and a hard lesson heeded by all involved. I do not doubt for a moment that once they acknowledge their actions and show genuine remorse, my son will restore their funding and return as a benefactor. How long this lasts will be entirely up to them, but I doubt they will go without for long. Until then, I will always ensure our dear Marigold has all she needs, physically, emotionally and spiritually.' Nellie reached across and embraced her, tears streaming down her face as Charlotte patted her on the back. 'Hush now, my dear friend. There is no need for tears. Floods of them were shed for many years and didn't help any of us then, and nor will they now. Marigold knows where home is and that the door is always open and that this is where she belongs amongst the people who love her—even if it is in secret.' Nellie nodded as she pulled away and attempted to regain her composure.

'Thank you for trusting me enough to tell me the truth. I never suspected a thing, even back then when Agnes was with child. I feel terrible how we all speculated for months over who sired the wean. Not once did anyone guess Reg.' Charlotte nodded, appearing pleased.

'I must retire shortly. Isabelle is arriving here early in the morning. She saw Mary and Anna off tonight, and I know her heart will be hurting as she has experienced so much loss, the poor darling. Poor Izzy is considering returning to Australia as she feels she has nothing left here now Magnolia is no longer with us. God rest the dear child. I still cry for sweet little Maggie, and I pray every night that Isabelle finds peace wherever she decides to go if she does choose to leave once again. At least she has that property, Willow Grove, she so adores, and she tells me the place is filled with people she loves and who love her back. There is even a young man there who has been her lover for the last five-years or so, who she speaks of with great affection. That can only be a good thing at our age. If the good Lord above grants me a few more years, I may even take a ship back there myself and see out my days beside her—and you will be with us, of course.'

Charlotte did not feel the need to confide in Nellie that Isabelle had been caring for the sisters in secret at one of the guest cottages on the grounds of Merinda Manor, where she had been staying for the last month. Nellie nodded as she rose to her feet, assisting Charlotte up, then linking arms before slowly making their way towards the door.

'It sounds like a wonderful place to see out our days together—just as we started our journey all those years ago in Australia, side by side. I've heard so many exciting stories from our dear Isabelle about the place over the last forty-years, and I cannot wait for the opportunity to go there and see it with my own eyes. They do say you should start as you mean to finish. Let's find Isabelle as soon as we wake to tell her.' Nellie smiled at her friend, her eyes twinkling as Charlotte nodded and smiled back before embracing her tightly, both grateful for all they had been given, but even more so for the people they had loved during this lifetime and who had loved them in return just as intensely, enveloping them in a rare and pure love that no amount of money, gold, or precious stones could ever buy.

A Word From The Author

THANK YOU FOR TAKING the time to read my series 'Samsara-The First Season'.' It's been nearly a decade since I wrote the first sentence of Abigail's story, and it is a privilege to share it with you. If you have a few moments, I would be deeply grateful if you left a review on your chosen platform or website. It will help other readers find books that they may never have discovered otherwise. Your feedback means the world to authors and we cannot thank you enough for your support!

Thank you for investing your valuable time and money in this story and I hope you enjoyed reading it.

If this series was not for you, that's perfectly okay. We all have different tastes as readers and we can't please everyone all the time. Thank you again for your support and I wish you well in finding novels that bring you joy. Much love to all xx

To find out more,
go to www.jlmartinauthor.com

About The Author

J. L. MARTIN LIVES in a quiet country town in Regional Victoria, Australia. In a past life of her own, she spent close to two decades working in the Welfare sector and at the coalface for the State Child Protection AHS Emergency Service as a lead investigator, applicant and expert witness within the Childrens' Court—both in the family and criminal divisions—along with the Family Law and Criminal Court systems, before being forced to retire with cumulative trauma as a result of a final assault sustained in the workplace while carrying out her duties. She holds a degree in welfare and has two adult daughters and four grandchildren — along with several adult foster daughters and grandchildren.

J L Martin's transition to full-time author began in December 2015 when she started writing as therapy to assist in her recovery from PTSD, ultimately leading to her debut series 'Samsara'.

Her only non-fiction book, 'A Journey to Finding YOUR New Normal—PTSD, Anxiety and Depression,' was first published in 2018; however, J L Martin recently updated the existing manuscript while adding a significant amount of new information due to a number of changes that have occurred in a short space of time, not only in her own life but more importantly within the mental health field—along with the irritating fact that the phrase 'New Normal' is now closely associated with Covid-19. The updated edition will be published under a new title, 'Sunshine after the Storm—Finding Joy after Trauma,' and is available on her website and from all good bookstores in ebook, paperback and audiobook from January 2022.

She owns a 19th-Century Coffee Palace & Bookstore with her partner, a creative soul and talented artist in his own right. Their 'Penny University,' stocks only tomes from Indie Authors to show their unwavering support of all writers within the community and around the world — and coffee — they have GREAT coffee.

Want to stay up to date and be the first to hear about Samsara? Go to jlmartinauthor.com to sign up for her newsletter and receive alerts and updates, along with bonus content from unpublished volumes. Links to social media and bookstores are available here too.

To find out more,

go to www.jlmartinauthor.com

SAMSARA

THE FIRST SEASON

START YOUR JOURNEY WITH Abigail in the epic new Australian historical fiction series spanning a lifetime. Based in Geelong, this debut series by J L Martin spans a lifetime, from 1890 to 1968. Join thousands of readers accompanying this cast of characters through each decade, sharing their joy and sorrow, their triumphs and tragedies, while trying to find out the meaning of the golden glow. Available in ebook, audiobook and paperback from all good bookstores and online platforms.

To find out more,
go to www.jlmartinauthor.com

The Golden Glow

SAMSARA-The First Season
Volume One Book One

What if you could remember a past life?
Or worse, what if you couldn't?

*B*ORN IN 1875 AND *raised in a Scottish orphan-age, Abigail is about to turn fifteen—an age where she will be cast out of the only home she has ever known—no matter how horrid. The day before* *they force her to leave behind the only life she has known to enter an uncertain future, a mysterious wooden box arrives requesting she travel to London to meet with a lawyer by the name of Henry Malcolm. Abigail is thrown into a world she is fearful of—while events from the past of which she has no control or influence could change the course of her life in ways she never expected. A reluctant journey taking her across the ocean to Melbourne, Australia, sees friendships formed that will last a lifetime—but leaves Abigail even more confused by the auras she has seen since she could first remember. Surprised by the golden glow surrounding many of the new souls she meets along the way, she wonders if they know something she doesn't. Only to find the further she travels from home, the more common they become, Abigail dives deeper into the mystery of these auras, soon discovering they could hold the answer to who she truly is—and what darkness hides in the past of which she has no control or influence.*

Unexpected Beginnings

SAMSARA-The First Season
Volume One Book Two

Abigail's journey to Melbourne, Australia, has blessed her with friendships that will last a lifetime—but has left her even more confused by the auras she has seen since she could first remember. Finding the further she travels from home, the more common they become, she is unable to confide in

another soul for fear of retribution. Feeling even more alone when she arrives in Geelong, Abigail finds all is not what it seemed or was promised. She is faced with an impossible choice that will impact her future—a future she feels she has no control over that leaves her torn between two very different men—forced to make a choice that will change her destiny in ways she could never have imagined.

Torn in Two

SAMSARA-The First Season
Volume One Book Three

Abigail makes her choice and marries the love of her life, leaving heartbreak behind and consequences that she must face in the future. Basking in the glow of her newfound life—a life so different from her time spent in the orphanage, it is unrecognisable to her as she tries to adjust to situations she has

never encountered before. Polly's past unexpectantly haunts them in this new land, leading to secrets being exposed and ending in murder. Abigail experiences a pleasant surprise, one that will change her life in ways she has never known, providing her with a sense of security and contentment she has never before experienced. However, unfavourable events soon unfold, leaving some of her friends, especially Dana, grieving and wishing they had never immigrated to Australia.

Loss of Innocence

SAMSARA-The First Season
Volume One Book Four

Abigail is the happiest she has ever been, feeling complete now she is surrounded by people who feel like family, a feeling she has never known before. Becoming a mother for the first time completes this new sense of belonging as she forges ahead and begins to make Willow Grove her own, running the prop-

erty on her own terms while discovering further information about the mysterious Great Aunt Isabelle. Her chef and best friend Leo continues to cause chaos and offense wherever he goes, a friendship Abigail cherishes despite him driving everyone else around him insane. Abigail is the happiest she has ever been; however, a gnawing fear inside her leaves her feeling confused, a fear she cannot shake despite having no foundation. Finally, Abigail comes face to face with the darkest dilemma of them all; an unknown past for which she is severely punished without a trial.

Unconditional Love

SAMSARA-The First Season
Volume One Book Five

Abigail and Aaron grieve for their stillborn twins, and the aftermath of the brutal attack on her leads to further trauma that will have life-changing consequences. Hamish remains a steadfast friend to both Abigail and Aaron, moving to Willow Grove permanently to help run the property, while Abi-

gail tries to keep life as normal as possible for those around her, particularly the twins, under impossible circumstances. Faced with the very real chance that she could lose someone she loves forever, she goes to extremes to keep them by her side, prepared to lose everything she owns to save those close to her.

Returning Home

SAMSARA-The First Season
Volume One Book Six

Abigail buries her soulmate and embarks on a journey to her homeland, desperate to return to the arms of her beloved Sister Josephine. Unfortunately, she is left feeling confused when the handsome Lord Harrington III makes her acquaintance on the journey, while Hamish has become a thorn in her

side, demanding her attention and love, which she is unable to give. Will Abigail be torn between two men yet again, and will she return to Australia with the twins after all that has happened and the memories Willow Grove holds? Only she can reconcile the unbearable pain she carries as she decides just where her heart belongs.

Letting Go

SAMSARA-The First Season
Volume One Book Seven

Abigail attempts to mend her broken heart by connecting to another, but questions if she truly has the ability to love again after losing Aaron.

Strong friendships are formed during their time abroad, the most significant with a soothsayer, Lilith Arcadia. Opening a door to the afterlife Abigail never considered existed, she discovers her connection to Aaron is not broken, only invisible, and life does indeed go on. And on. And on.

Soul Connections

SAMSARA-The First Season
Volume One Book Eight

War breaks out, and Abigail is left to manage Willow Grove while the men she loves fight for their country, leaving her to console those who have lost while suffering her own torment.

Abigail meets Sarah Stewart, and a deep friendship is established, bringing a very special child into her life who will change the course of her future. Abigail again faces one of the most traumatic events of her life, leaving her unable to cope or find peace, despite a loved soul on the other side showing themselves to her and revealing some interesting information about the golden glow.

Healing The Heart

SAMSARA-The First Season
Volume One Book Nine

Abigail returns to Scotland to visit the orphanage where she has helped change the lives of the girls left in their care; however, parting for the last time from those she loves leaves her grieving deeply. Maslow leaves a final word for her, which shakes her to the core, taking away the only peace she had left. Sadie

moves to Willow Grove, and it is only when her first child is born Abigail finally understands the true meaning of the golden glow.

Legacy and Love

SAMSARA-The First Season
Volume One Book Ten

Polly and Catherine prove to be steadfast friends who see Abigail safely into an unknown future, while she reflects on her life and tries to make some sense of it all, finally realising that no amount of money can protect you from tragedy or the obstacles sent to test us all. The birth of a child has a shocking

consequence, leaving Abigail stunned and unsure how she will ever move forward or reconnect with those she loves.

Leo-Back to Me!

SAMSARA-The First Season
Volume One Book Eleven

Leo Currenti is a famous chef working at The Rialto Hotel in London in 1889. Leo, a unique man with a hilarious personality, believes he is the only really important person in the world and should be treated accordingly. A man of mystery, he holds many secrets close, not allowing anyone other than

those he deeply loves to know his true heart. His kitchen falls into chaos when a murder occurs at the hotel, and subsequent murders after that, threatening his sense of security and jeopardising not only his job but his life. Thrown into a web of lies and deceit that are not of his own making, he tries to live the best life that he can, always shocking and entertaining people with what comes out of his mouth along the way!

Join Leo on his journey through the last year he spent in London before meeting Abigail, who changed the course of his life. The secrets of his past are finally revealed in this hilarious novel, while also delving deeper into the serious side of Leo, a side no one knew he had!

Lilith-Utopia

SAMSARA-The First Season
Volume One Book Twelve

It's 1905, and Jasper and Lilith Arcadia have left everything they owned in London to start a commune in Australia. They never fitted into their aristocratic upbringings and brought shame on their families for the friends they kept and the lives they lived, with Lilith being a soothsayer, a seer, a psychic

to the wealthy and famous of England and Europe. With a large sum of money provided to them by their families, Jasper and Lilith buy a property in Western Victoria and name it Utopia, attracting like-minded people who refuse to abide by society's expectations. It is Jasper and Lilith's unconventional life that suddenly seems normal compared to the people Utopia attracts. It takes some time for Lilith to become accustomed to her new life; however, she finds beauty in things others barely look at. It is when she finds beauty in another man real trouble begins for Jasper and Lilith. When tragedy strikes and brother starts to suspect brother, decisions need to finally be made, some with heartbreaking consequences.

Join Lilith as she embarks on her new life in Australia, a journey through the first year as she settles into a vastly different environment from what she's accustomed to, unaware her heart would never be the same, or how her actions, and those of others living alongside her would change the course of events and the paths of their descendants for generations to come.

Acknowledgements

FOREMOST, I WOULD LIKE to thank my editor and narrator, Marianne Delaforce. Not only does she polish my words until they shine—without her 'Samsara' would not be available as an audiobook. Thank you, beautiful soul. Not unlike the plot of this series, you entered my life serendipitously and I am grateful to call you a friend. Bless you.

My book cover designer, Thea Atkinson, what can I say? You are the most beautiful soul, and your work is fantastic. They say don't judge a book by its cover... but how can you not when they are just so lovely? Thank you. Your talent and generosity is appreciated.

You have a heart of service and a generous spirit, Stuart Grant. For no reason other than that, you helped a stranger. Thank you for designing my beautiful website and teaching me how to use it. Your patience was noted and appreciated. You are seriously my hero and one day; I hope to meet you and your sweet family. I'm grateful.

To my dad, the one constant in my life who doesn't see me as weird and supports everything I do. I love you.

To my mum, I love you too.

To Steve, my love, my heart, my best friend and my favourite human. I adore you and love you without limitation or conditions.

To Ava, Thomas and Isla... just because I love you, too.

Aurorah, Jakobie, Audrey and Makenzie, I love you to the moon and back.

To my beautiful friends. You know who you are. Thank you for your support in every way, on every level. Without you, I wouldn't have had the confidence to come this far... and you were the ones who took time out of your busy lives to read the series and push me to publish. You are forever loved and appreciated.

To my Beta Readers—Gailene Cuttler, Ruben Panopio, Vicki Howard and Michelle Norman. Thank you for your input and love of Samsara. Your feedback has shaped this series. Much love.

To my readers. What can I say, other than thank you for becoming so involved and passionate about my series. You encouraged me. You gave me the confidence to believe in myself. You told all your friends about 'Samsara', bringing thousands of readers who connected to the books and characters, embracing them as family. I am grateful for each and every one of you and always will be.

Wanting More?

Exciting new contemporary crime trilogy

"Spawned of Sin Trilogy"

by

JL MARTIN

Time Travellers Publishing House PTY LTD

Through Windows in the Sky I Fall

BOOK ONE

MOLLY MAE HAS EMBARKED on a new journey in the opposite direction of where she'd once been headed and was unknowingly predestined to go due to the sins of her forefathers. Relocating to Melbourne to start a new life after a decade of medicating her emotional pain in ways she wished she hadn't, she didn't regret for a moment leaving behind the community in which she was raised—along with the horror and humiliation of her father, Michael Mae's, arrest ten years before, exposing him as the countries most prolific serial killer since white man first stepped foot on Australian soil and bellowed *Terra Nullius*.

Having battled substance abuse since the age of fifteen and tormented by her own secrets and demons, she has turned her back on her previous life and is determined to make a fresh start away from the small town gossip, hate filled stares and constant harassment from those who still treated her family no different from if they killed these women with their own hands. Moving from the tiny country town where she was born in rural Victoria to study Social Work at the prestigious Melbourne University, Molly tentatively forms new friendships with an eclectic mix of souls, but soon the reappearance of old friends and foes leaves her shaken and unable to think straight.

Within hours of arriving at her new building, Molly finds herself the sole witness to a murder, setting off a chain reaction that brings up old wounds and the shocking realisation that no matter how far you run, you can never truly escape the past—or the ties that bind through blood, generational sin and soul connections.

James Cavanaugh, now a Detective Sergeant in the homicide squad, is head of the Taskforce responsible to investigate what initially appears to be an open and shut case—but a new wave of killings centred in Molly's building sends them on a heart-stopping race against time in this intense psychological thriller that will have you guessing right until the very last page.

'Through Windows In The Sky I Fall' is the first novel in this exciting new contemporary crime trilogy **'Spawned Of Sin'** by J L Martin, author of the epic Australian historical fantasy fiction series, **'Samsara-The First Season'**.

Tainted Blood, Poisoned Soul

BOOK TWO

F IVE YEARS ON, AND the invisible killer is serving four life sentences at Barwon Prison for the murders at the hotel in 2020—alongside Molly's biological father, imprisoned a decade and a half before. *Tainted Blood, Poisoned Soul,* explores the long hidden secrets and crimes of Michael Mae as he reflects on his life in storytelling to his cellmates, whom he feels understand and accept him—one more so than the others. But do they?

Are they really cut from the same cloth as Australia's most notorious serial killer?

Molly, now a qualified Social Worker after graduating from Melbourne University with honours, asks herself the same question every single day. And she still hasn't found an answer. Employed as a lead investigator with Child Protective Services, she works closely with police task forces and within the judicial system, much to her indignation. Living in the seaside suburb of St Kilda where she purchased her first real home all on her own, she feels she finally belongs somewhere with her 'tribe', an eclectic and often hilarious cast of characters.

She no longer has to work to survive, but having money doesn't stop her springing out of bed before dawn every day with a fire in her belly and a passion long dead in most of her colleagues who'd spent any longer than five years in the job. She wanted to make a difference. It's only when she comes face to face with Braven for the first time since they parted fifteen years before, she begins to doubt if she can really help anyone when she feels powerless in saving her own son from himself—and it seems, someone around him who is murdering young people living in out-of-home care.

Will the love of family—and friends who've become family—protect Molly from danger lurking close by, so insidious it's unrecognisable even to the intuitive?

Jump on board and come on this thrilling, white knuckled ride as Detective Sergeant James Cavanaugh and his squad race against time to not only stop the Resi Ripper preying on the most vulnerable, but protect those closer to home they never imagined would be at risk.

'Tainted Blood, Poisoned Soul' is the second book in this exciting new contemporary crime trilogy ***'Spawned Of Sin'*** by J L Martin, author of the epic Australian historical fantasy fiction series, ***'Samsara-The First Season.'***

The Ties That Bind Behind Me

BOOK THREE

MOLLY MAE IS ABOUT to turn fifty. Married for just over fifteen years, she needs a break from raising rambunctious, entitled teenagers, a stale relationship, and a job taking up far too much of her time and energy to do anything else well—or even adequately. What's worse, she recently relapsed and is so ashamed, she can't even admit to herself she's spiraling out of control and needs help. Those close suspect her deep depression and miserable countenance stems from recent events she clearly resented her husband for—but refused to speak of it even with her closest confidants. Her husband, supportive but frustrated over her recent erratic behaviour and her all-or-nothing attitude, suggests she take a holiday with her friends—overseas if that's what it takes to get her to relax and unplug from the turmoil that's plagued them over the last year. Reluctantly agreeing and hoping to address her addiction in private while away, Molly heads to Tasmania—as far across the water as she's prepared to go when she could be needed at home or work—along with Scott and Tiffany, who cheerfully leave their own kids at home for their partners to deal with without a backward glance, or a drop of guilt. It doesn't take long before June joins them, bringing someone from Molly's past, and soon after, fellow travellers around them—some familiar, some not—turn up murdered one by one, seemingly with no connection. But is there? And why are the signs of guilt all pointing to Molly, no matter where anyone stands or what direction they look in?

Join us on the final journey in this series as Tasmanian homicide detectives move swiftly to solve a string of killings that could have so easily gone unnoticed, if not for one common link—Molly Mae.

'The Ties That Bind Behind Me' is the third and final book in this exciting new contemporary psychological thriller trilogy ***'Spawned Of Sin'*** by J L Martin, author of the epic Australian historical fantasy fiction series, ***'Samsara-The First Season.'***